NO DRAGONS
ON MY QUILT

PRESENTED TO

BY

ON

Additional copies of this book may be ordered from: American Quilter's Society
P.O. Box 3290, Paducah, KY 42002-3290 @$12.95. Add $1.00 for postage & handling.
10 9 8 7 6 5 4 3 2 1

Library of Congress Cataloging-in-Publication Data
Laury, Jean Ray
No dragons on my quilt/by Jean Ray Laury; with Ritva Laury and Lizabeth Laury.
p.   cm.
Summary: When Benjamin is afraid to go to bed by himself, he is comforted by the special quilt his grandmother makes for him.
Includes instructions and patterns for making the quilt featured in the story.
ISBN: 0-89145-967-7: $12.95
[1. Quilts–Fiction. 2. Grandmothers–Fiction. 3. Bedtime–Fiction. 4. Fear–Fiction.] I. Laury, Ritva. II. Laury, Lizabeth. III. Title.
PZ7.L377No 1990   [E]–dc20   90-46237

NO DRAGONS ON MY QUILT

by JEAN RAY LAURY

with RITVA LAURY
and LIZABETH LAURY

*Patterns and
instructions for
making the quilt in
the story begin on
page 32.*

American Quilter's Society
P.O. Box 3290, Paducah, KY 42002-3290

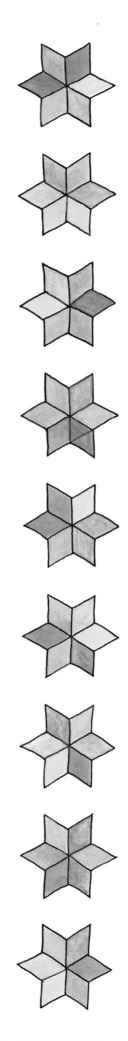

Benjamin went to visit his grandmother.
He liked being at her house
With the bedroom upstairs
And the cookie jar on a low shelf in the kitchen.

What he DIDN'T like was going to bed at night
When he was all alone.

Then Benjamin's eyes got as round as the moon.

6

"Grandma," he called…"Grandma,
I need one more story….Then I can go to sleep."

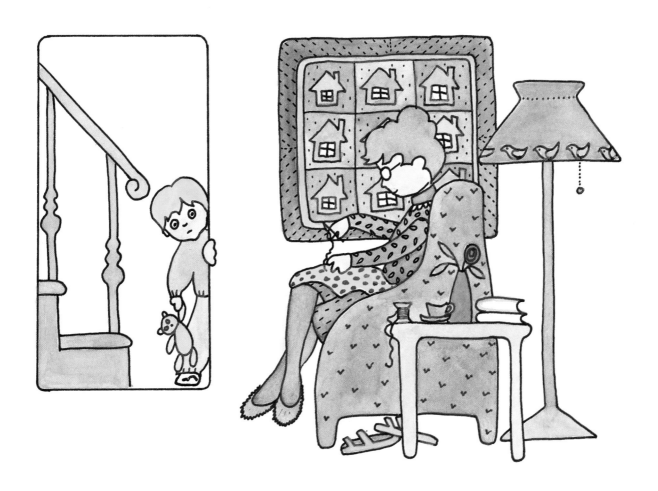

So she read him one more story.
"Now, off to bed," she said.
And she tucked him in and hugged him
And said good night.

"Grandma," he called, "Grandma,
I need one more drink of water....
Then I can go to sleep."

So she gave him one more drink of water.
"Now, off to bed," she said.
And then she tucked him in and kissed him
And said good night.

"Grandma," he called. "Grandma,
I need one more little cookie....
Then I can go to sleep."

So Grandma brought the cookie jar
And let Benjamin reach in for one more cookie.

"Now, off to bed," she said.
And she tucked him in.

12

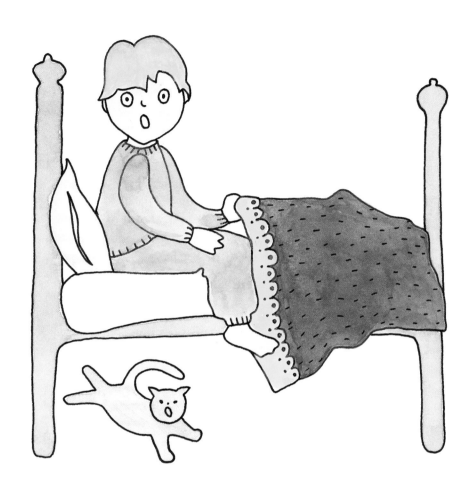

"Grandma, oh Grandma,
I think I left my toys outside.
I'd better bring them in.
Then I can go to sleep."

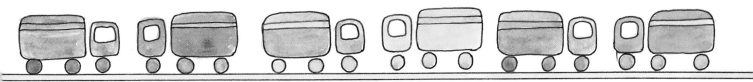

So Benjamin and his grandmother went outside to look.
No toys were in the back yard.
No toys were in the front yard.

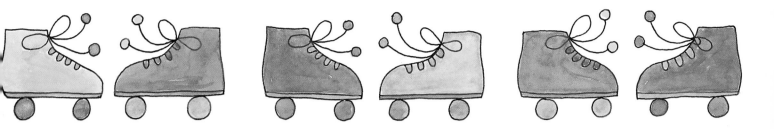

All the toys had been put in the garage.

"Oh," said Benjamin. "I guess I forgot."

"Now, off to bed," his grandmother said.
"And this is the last time."

And she tucked him in and said good night.

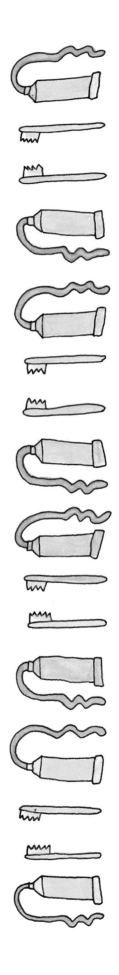

"Grandma," he called. "Grandma,
I need to brush my teeth.
Then I can go to sleep."

17

So they found his toothbrush
And Benjamin squeezed out the toothpaste
And he brushed his teeth.
"Now, off to bed," she said.
And she tucked him in.

"Grandma," he called. "Oh, Grandma,
I think I hear a noise!
I think a dragon is coming to get my bear."

"I think a dragon is coming to get...ME!"

So his grandmother
Leaned out the window
And looked
But she saw no dragons.

Then Benjamin
Leaned out the window
And looked
And he didn't see
Any dragons either.

20

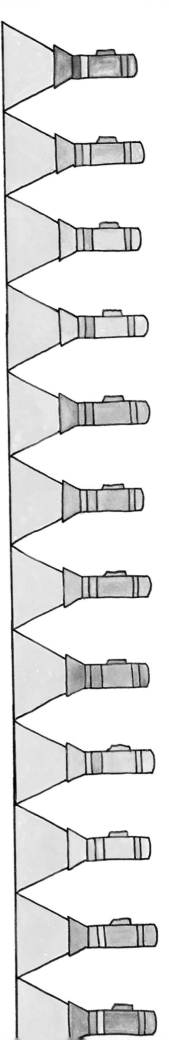

His grandmother leaned out the window one more time
And looked again.
There were no dragons anywhere.

"Now, off to bed!" she said.

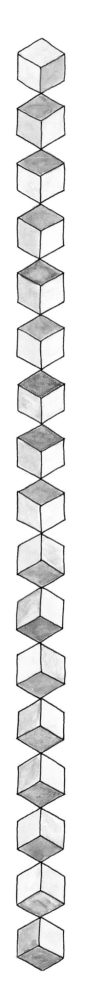

"Grandma," called Benjamin, "Oh, Grandma,
I need some company.
Then I can go to sleep."

And his grandmother said, "I know just the thing you need.
You need a quilt!"

"A what?" asked Benjamin. "A quilt?"

"Yes," said his grandmother, "A quilt."

"Bring me my sewing basket," said his grandmother.
And she took all her scraps of cloth out of the basket.

23

And from one scrap of fabric she cut a sailboat,
And she sewed it on a piece of cloth.

Then she cut out the shapes
For a glass of water
And she sewed them on
Another piece of cloth.

Next she cut out cookies and cocoa.
Then a toothbrush
And a roller skate
And an apple and a truck
And ice cream cones,
A flashlight,
And, of course, a teddy bear.

She sewed and sewed the cloth shapes
Until every picture was done.

Then Benjamin's grandmother laid all the pictures
Out on the floor to see how they looked.
She added squares of red and green and strips of blue.

Then she sewed all the pieces of cloth together.
She sewed and sewed and sewed some more
And she quilted and quilted and quilted
Until the whole quilt was done.

"There," said Benjamin's grandmother. "There is your quilt."
And she wrapped it around Benjamin.
It felt all warm and snuggly
And fluffy. It felt just right.

"This quilt," she said,
"Has everything you need...
Your book, a drink of water,
Some cookies, a toothbrush,
All your toys, and the sun,
The moon and the stars."

Benjamin yawned.

"Grandma," he whispered, "Grandma,
Are there any dragons on my quilt?"

Benjamin's grandmother held the quilt up
And looked very carefully all over the top of the quilt.
And she looked very carefully all over the back of the quilt.

"No, Benjamin," she said.
"There are no dragons on your quilt."

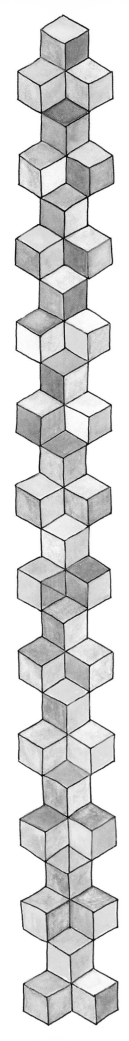

"Good," said Benjamin.
"No dragons on my quilt."

And he snuggled down on his pillow,
Deep under his new quilt.

And said good night.

And Benjamin went right to sleep.

The End

MAKING YOUR OWN
QUILT WITH NO DRAGONS ON IT

Any child would be delighted to sleep beneath this quilt, so general instructions for making it are included on the following pages. Directions for both appliqueing and quick stenciling the blocks are included.

The designs can also be used as patterns for embroidering or for drawing on fabric. Children's projects might include cutting the shapes from colored paper and punching the blocks with holes along the edges so that they can be laced together with yarn or ribbon to make a paper quilt. Individual designs can be applied to pillows, pajamas or tote bags.

Regardless of the method you select, have fun!

PREPARATION

FABRICS NEEDED

Blue	1⅝ yards
Red	1½ yards
Green	1⅓ yards
White	1¼ yards for blocks (this allows no extra for error or stencil practice)
Backing	52" x 60" (or 3 yards if it is pieced once across the width of the quilt)

CUTTING OUT THE QUILT

Note: All measurements are for finished sizes. Add your seam allowance to all cut edges.

Blocks: Cut 16 fabric rectangles, 7" x 9". Each will finish at 7" x 9", so be sure to add your seam allowance to these measurements. On the pattern pages, the broken line around each block indicates the stitching line and the solid line the cut edge of the block. If you plan to use quick-stencil, you might want to cut several extra blocks to use for practice.

When the blocks are completed (whether appliqued or stenciled) you will need to cut binding, sashing, borders and backing as follows:

Binding:
 Cut 2, 56" x 3" in blue
 Cut 2, 48" x 3" in blue
 (Cut these on the lengthwise grain.
 Cut before cutting the sashing strips.)

Sashing:
 Cut 20, 7" x 2" in blue
 Cut 20, 9" x 2" in blue
 Cut 25, 2" x 2" (13 red & 12 green)

1st Border:
 Cut 2, 1¼" x 46" in green (for sides)
 Cut 2, 1¼" x 40½" in green (for top & bottom)

2nd Border:
 Cut 2, 3" x 48½" in red (for sides)
 Cut 2, 3" x 46½" in red (for top & bottom)

Backing:
 Cut 1, 52" x 60". (This measurement includes an allowance of several inches on each edge, to be trimmed after quilting.) It may be necessary to seam two pieces of fabric.

MAKING THE BLOCKS

The blocks can be appliqued or quick stenciled. Directions for both methods follow.The patterns are identical for the two methods, but for applique a few of the shapes are handled differently. Tips for handling the specific shapes in each block are included on the pattern pages.

USING THE APPLIQUE METHOD:

Turn to the pattern section and trace the pieces for each block or copy on a copy machine. When you cut your fabric pieces, remember that each pattern is shown finished size, so you will need to add seam allowance to all cut edges. Cotton fabrics will be easier to applique than fabrics which are partly synthetic. When you have your pieces cut, lay out the pieces for the block, position them, and then use either a running stitch or blindstitch to applique them in place. Helpful shortcuts and hints are found on each pattern page. When you have finished the blocks, turn to the finishing directions on page 35.

USING THE QUICK-STENCIL METHOD:

Preparing the Stencils

The quick-stencil method involves ironing freezer paper stencils to the fabric to mask out areas that are to remain unpainted. This method is fast and simple. For each block of the quilt you will need several pieces of freezer paper – one piece for each different color. Cut the freezer paper into sheets the size of the quilt block.

Trace the design for a single color onto the piece of freezer paper, drawing on the dull side. (The shiny side will be ironed to the surface of the fabric.) Remove the freezer paper from the pattern, label it, set it aside, and then do the same thing for each additional color, using a new sheet for each new color.

When the shapes to be made in each color have been traced, use a craft knife or trimming scissors to cut out each shape to be painted on the fabric. Then iron one freezer-paper stencil on the fabric, aligning the corners. Use a medium hot iron to fuse the paper to the fabric. Special care must be taken to adhere the inside edges of the cut shapes.

Painting the Shapes

Have a smooth absorbent work surface available (newsprint or a smooth cardboard is good). Use any permanent textile paint which is water soluble when wet and is set by heat. These paints are about the consistency of sour cream and will be easy to work with.

Color can be applied with a stencil brush or stiff-bristle brush (by brushing colors from the cut edges towards the center) or with a scraper or squeegee (by spreading the paint).

In the second method, a small amount of paint (about a half teaspoon for smaller shapes) is placed on the adhered freezer-paper, about an inch away from the cutout design where fabric is exposed. The paint must then be spread over the open area of the design. Spreading is accomplished by using a plastic squeegee (sometimes used in screen printing) or a sharp plastic blade such as a plasterer's tool, or a flexible spatula. In lieu of these tools, a credit card will work well. Spread the paint smoothly over the opening, so that the color is evenly distributed. Avoid scraping the tool directly into the cut edges of the paper. Once spread, the excess paint is placed back in the paint jar and the fabric is left to dry (or partially dry). When it can be handled, the paper is carefully peeled off, revealing the design. It should then be heat-set before a second color is added.

Align each new stencil, matching page corners and the printed shapes, and then stencil that color on. In some cases it will be easier to print one shape over another rather than to attempt getting two shapes to match perfectly. Some helpful short cuts and hints accompany each drawing.

Heat-Setting the Color:

Test the textile paints you have selected by trying a stencil on a sample of your fabric. Follow the instructions that come with your paints. Usually, for heat setting a medium hot iron must be used directly on the dried painted surface. About 15 to 20 seconds of heat is usually adequate to set the dye to permanence. The finished piece is then washable. Test your printed fabric by heat-setting it and then washing it. The finish on some fabrics may resist the color. A longer drying time before washing will result in a more permanent color on some fabrics.

Trouble-Shooting:

If you find paint has smeared beyond the cut edges when you pull the freezer paper away, it may result from:
a. edges which have been inadequately ironed down
b. paint which has been scraped into the cut edges (and forced under them)

Solution:
a. iron edges more carefully
b. use a warmer iron to adhere freezer paper
c. scrape paint from cut edges toward center
d. check the work surface to be sure it is smooth
e. try more padding (newspaper or flannel over cardboard) under the fabric you are printing.

If you find streaked color, it may result from:
a. an inadequate amount of paint, meaning that several passes of the squeegee were necessary
b. paint colors that were not thoroughly mixed
c. an uneven work surface (corrugated cardboard, for example, will produce lines in the print)
d. wrinkled or unironed fabric

Solution:
a. place more paint on the freezer paper before printing
b. mix colors more thoroughly
c. press all fabrics
d. work on a smooth surface

If you find colors run when your sample block is washed, it may result from:
a. not allowing the paint to dry thoroughly
b. inadequate heat-setting
c. printing on fabric which was not prewashed
d. using a fabric with a finish which prevents the color from penetrating

Solution:
a. dry painted fabric for at least one day before heat-setting
b. set with a hotter iron for a longer period of time
c. prewash fabric
d. try another fabric (all cotton, untreated will work best)
e. check paint labels for specific instructions for the brand of paint you are using

ASSEMBLING THE QUILT TOP

Arrange the finished blocks, sashing strips and squares as shown in the photo on the back cover. Join the top row of four blocks using five of the longer sashing strips (joining the 9" (plus seam allowances) sashing to the 9" (plus seam allowances) side of the block).

Repeat for all four rows. Press seams open.

Next, using four of the shorter sashing strips and five of the sashing squares, make a horizontal band of sashing. Be sure you have alternated red and green squares as shown in the back cover photo.

Repeat for all five rows. Press seams open.

Pin a row of the horizontal sashing strips to a row of blocks, carefully matching seams. Keep all seams open. Repeat until the quilt is assembled. Press.

Add the 46" (green) borders to the sides of the quilt, then the 40½" to the bottom and top. Next add the 48½" (red) borders to the sides of the quilt, then the 46½" to the bottom and top.

Press seams carefully so that the colored fabric is pressed away from the white blocks. Keeping seams open will prevent colored threads from appearing under the white squares.

QUILTING THE FINISHED TOP

Set the quilt top with backing and batting into a quilting frame or, to quilt with a hoop or on a table top, assemble as follows:

Place the quilt backing on a smooth surface, with the right side facing down. If your smooth surface is a floor or table, tape each edge in several places to keep the backing smooth. (On carpeting, pin the edges instead of taping). Place a thin layer of batting over the backing. Then place the quilt top over the batting, right side up.

Baste, starting at the center and working towards the edges, in horizontal, vertical and diagonal lines. Baste about every three inches and at the outside edge.

Quilt horizontal and vertical lines through the sashings and borders. Then quilt individual blocks, using the pattern suggested in the quilting diagram on page 52. Use a similar quilting pattern on the other blocks. A light blue quilting thread was used in the cover quilt. When quilting is completed, carefully trim the batting and backing to the finished top size.

ADDING THE BINDING

Prepare binding by folding it in half lengthwise, with the wrong sides of the fabric together. Press. Then place the 56" length of folded binding on the face of the quilt at one side, with the raw edges of the binding matching the raw edge of the quilt top. Pin or baste and stitch on the seam line. About ½" of extra binding is allowed at each end, so after sewing, trim each end of the binding flush with the top and bottom. Repeat for other side. Next add top and bottom bindings in the same way, allowing ¾" extra at each end. Fold the excess allowance of top and bottom bindings over the side bindings. Hand stitch the folded edge of the binding to the seam line on the back of the quilt.

SIGN AND DATE YOUR QUILT

Enjoy!

COCOA AND COOKIES

APPLIQUE: Cut handle and cup as two separate pieces. Sew handle first; then let cup overlap raw edges of handle. Use a printed fabric for the cup or add details with permanent marker. Simplify cookies to circular shapes.

QUICK-STENCIL: Paint cup first, then the details. Steam and cookies are added last.

CAKE

APPLIQUE: Sew saucer as an oval to be over-lapped by cake. Cut the cake as a single large yellow shape; then overlap the frosting on top of it.

QUICK-STENCIL: Print cake sections first, then frosting, and the saucer and spoon last.

TRUCK

APPLIQUE: Sew highway lines in place first; then add truck. Do wheels last. Window can be applied on top rather than cut out.

QUICK-STENCIL: Paint highway lines, the truck. Do wheels last.

APPLIQUE: Cut raindrops
from synthetic suede
or enlarge the drops
so that they can be
more easily sewn.

MOON AND STARS

APPLIQUE: Since small stars are difficult to applique, cut them from synthetic suede or embroider them. The moon could be applied as a full circle with the profile embroidered over the top. Embroider the eye and cheek.

QUICK-STENCIL:
Print moon first, features.
Print stars last.

APPLE

APPLIQUE: Stem will be more easily accomplished with embroidery.

QUICK-STENCIL: Print apple first, then stem and leaves.

TOOTHBRUSH

APPLIQUE: Embroider the
hole in the toothbrush as
it is too small to sew easily.

QUICK-STENCIL: Print tube
first, then brush and tube
end, adding bristles and
puddle next, and paste last.

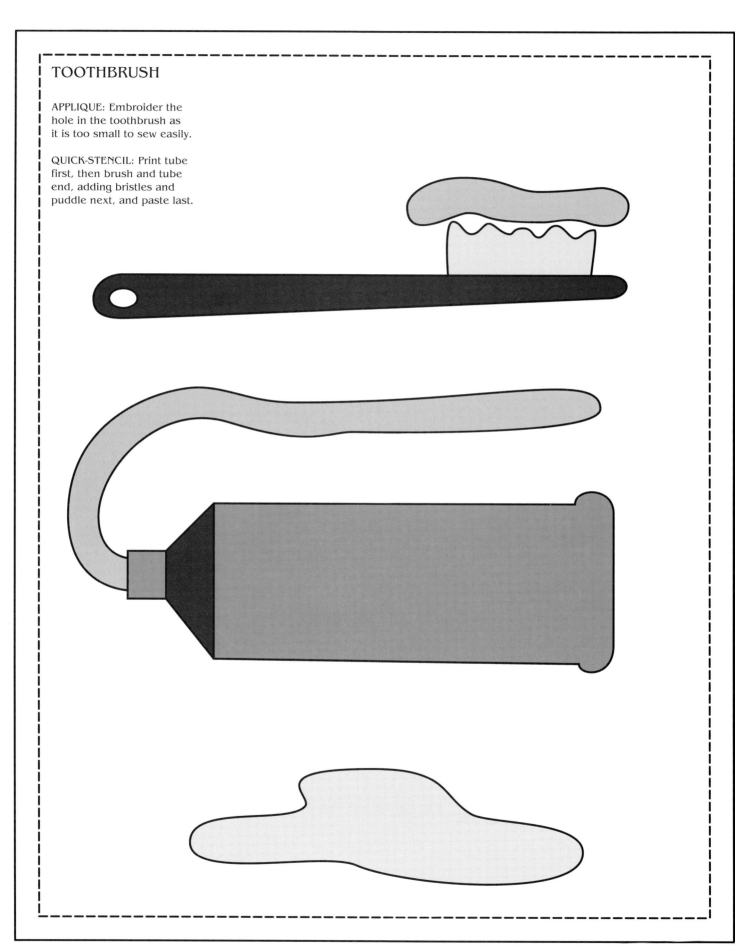

CANDLE

APPLIQUE: Sew large circle of flame first, then second circle, and next the flame itself and the wick. Then do the candle-holder, suggesting the ring with embroidery, or eliminating it. Finally, add the candle, overlapping candle-holder.

QUICK-STENCIL: Do the large circle as a solid circle, place the second circle over that, then the flame and the wick last.

ICE CREAM CONES

APPLIQUE: Sew sides of cones in place, leaving cone tops open. Then overlap ice cream onto the top of the cone. Add cherry stem and cherry chunks with embroidery or use a red polka dot fabric to suggest texture.

QUICK-STENCIL: Work from bottom up, starting with cones, then the ice cream, and finally the second dip or the cherry.

ROLLER SKATE

APPLIQUE: Sew shoe in place first. Laces may be embroidered, cut from synthetic suede or made by sewing on an actual shoelace.

QUICK-STENCIL: Print shoe first, then lace and ties over the top of shoe. Do wheels last.

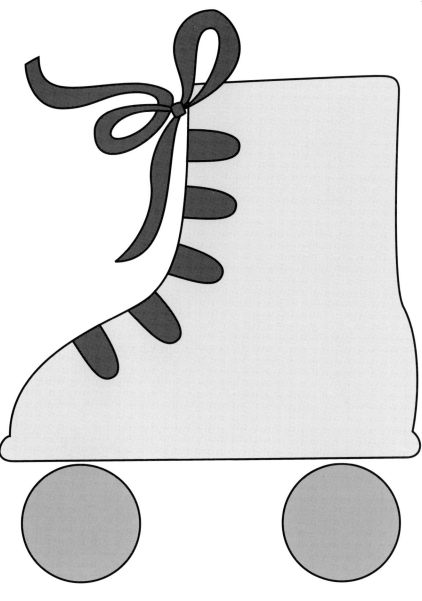

FLASHLIGHT

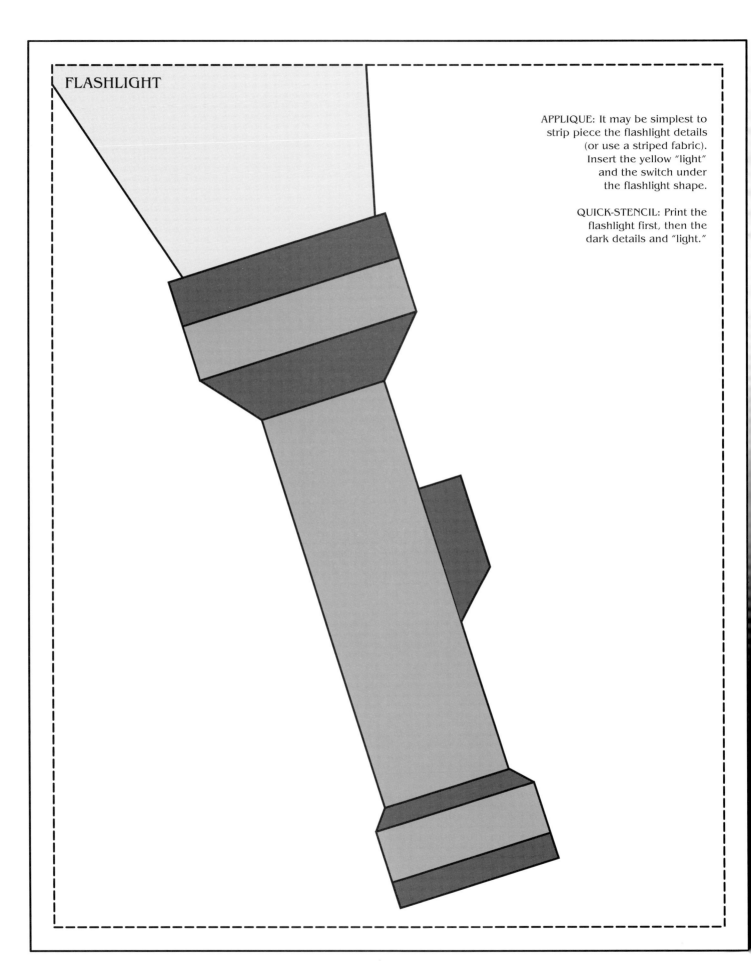

APPLIQUE: It may be simplest to strip piece the flashlight details (or use a striped fabric). Insert the yellow "light" and the switch under the flashlight shape.

QUICK-STENCIL: Print the flashlight first, then the dark details and "light."

APPLIQUE: Simplify sewing of the radiating lines by substituting long narrow rectangles for the triangles (or blunt the points of the triangles). Then applique a large circle over the wide open ends of the radiating shapes. Sew second circle over the first.

QUICK-STENCIL: Paint large circle and radiating points as one shape; then add the small circle on top.

GLASS

APPLIQUE: Sew glass shape first;
then add white area, eliminating
the "waves" on top. Sew straw last.
Fabric can be accordion folded
to suggest bend in straw.

QUICK-STENCIL: Print glass first,
then straw.

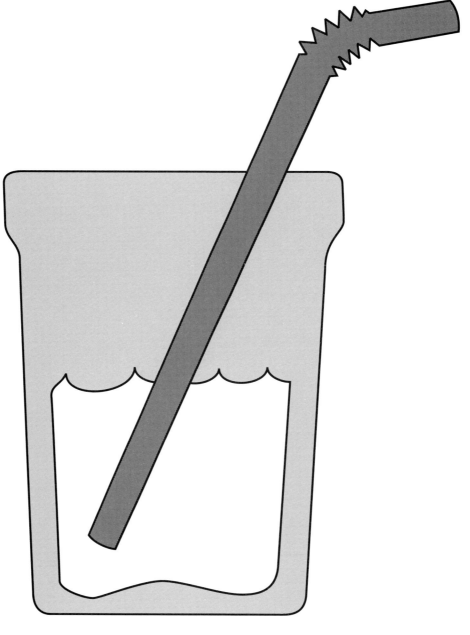

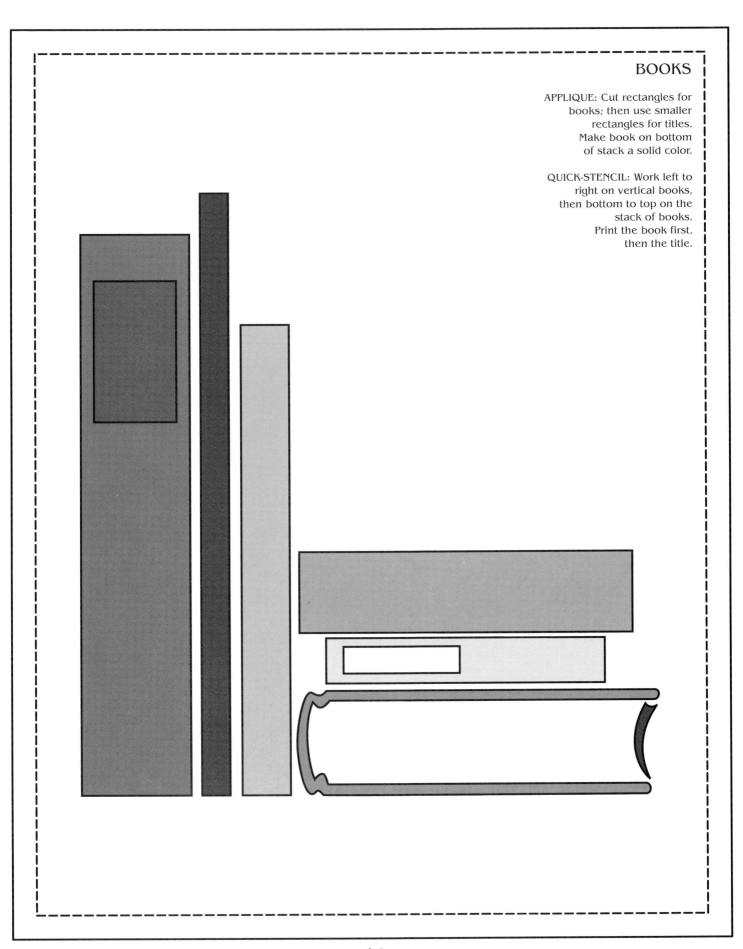

BOOKS

APPLIQUE: Cut rectangles for books; then use smaller rectangles for titles. Make book on bottom of stack a solid color.

QUICK-STENCIL: Work left to right on vertical books, then bottom to top on the stack of books. Print the book first, then the title.

TEDDY BEAR

APPLIQUE: Sew arms and legs first. Then overlap body, head, and the vest last. Cut ears, face details and paws from synthetic suede or other non-woven material that will not need to be turned under (or add details with permanent marker or embroidery).

QUICK-STENCIL: Print light gold (head and limbs) first, then dark gold body, details and red vest.

BOAT

APPLIQUE: Sew boat, then sails. Add flag with applique or embroidery. Cut waves from synthetic suede or simplify the applique by using a band of blue to suggest water.

QUICK-STENCIL: Print boat first, then sails, flag and waves.

P.S. Don't forget to check to make certain that there are no dragons on your quilt!